RAINBOW magic

The Weather Fairies

Thanks to real fairies
everywhere

Special thanks to
Sue Bentley

ORCHARD BOOKS
96 Leonard Street, London EC2A 4XD
Orchard Books Australia
32/45-51 Huntley Street, Alexandria, NSW 2015
A Paperback Original
First published in Great Britain in 2004
Rainbow Magic is a registered trademark of Working Partners Limited
Series created by Working Partners Limited, London W6 0QT
Text © Working Partners Limited 2004
Illustrations © Georgie Ripper 2004
The right of Georgie Ripper to be identified as the illustrator
of this work has been asserted by her in accordance
with the Copyright, Designs and Patents Act, 1988.
A CIP catalogue record for this book is available
from the British Library.
ISBN 1 84362 636 5
9 10
Printed in China

Evie
the Mist
Fairy

by Daisy Meadows

illustrated by Georgie Ripper

ORCHARD BOOKS

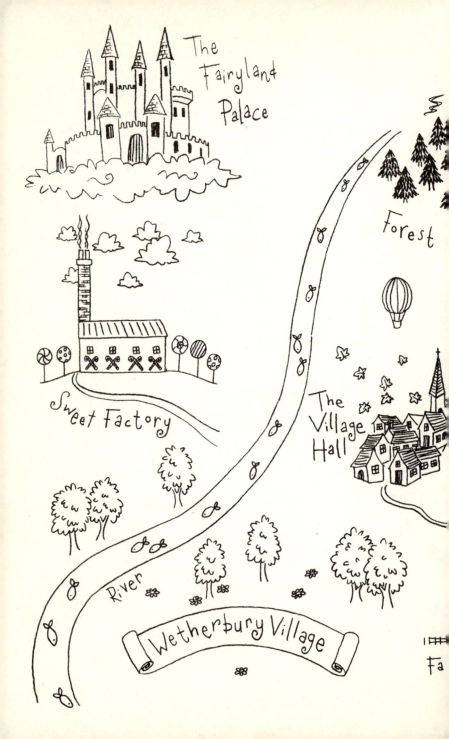

The Fairyland Palace

Forest

Sweet Factory

The Village Hall

River

Wetherbury Village

Fa

Goblins green and goblins small,
I cast this spell to make you tall.
As high as the palace you shall grow.
My icy magic makes it so.

Then steal Doodle's magic feathers,
Used by the fairies to make all weathers.
Climate chaos I have planned
On Earth, and here, in Fairyland!

Contents

A Misty Morning

"Wake up, sleepy head!" cried Kirsty
Tate to her friend, Rachel, as she jumped
out of bed and started to dress.

Rachel Walker was asleep in the spare
bed in Kirsty's room. She was staying
with Kirsty and her parents in the village
of Wetherbury. Sleepily, she rolled over
and opened her eyes. "I was dreaming

that we were back in Fairyland," she told Kirsty. "The weather was topsy-turvy – sunny and snowing all at the same time – and Doodle was trying to sort it out." Doodle, the fairies' magic weather cockerel, had been on Rachel's mind a lot lately, because she and Kirsty were on an important fairy mission!

Each day in Fairyland, with the help of the Weather Fairies, Doodle used his magic tail feathers to organise the weather. Each of the seven magic feathers controlled a different kind of weather, and each of the seven Weather Fairies was responsible for working with one feather in particular. The system worked perfectly until mean old Jack Frost sent seven goblins to steal Doodle's magic feathers.

The goblins ran off into the human world with one feather each, and when poor Doodle followed them out of Fairyland, he found himself transformed into a rusty metal weather-vane. The Queen of the Fairies had asked Rachel and Kirsty to help find the magic feathers and return them to Doodle.

Meanwhile, Fairyland's weather was all mixed up – and the goblins had been using the feathers to cause weather chaos in the human world too.

"Poor Doodle," Kirsty said, looking out 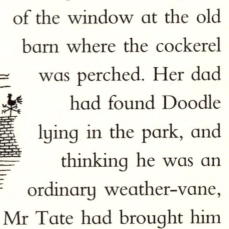 of the window at the old barn where the cockerel was perched. Her dad had found Doodle lying in the park, and thinking he was an ordinary weather-vane, Mr Tate had brought him home and put him on the barn roof.

"Hopefully we'll find another magic feather today," Kirsty continued. "We've already found four of the stolen feathers. We just need to find the other three and then Doodle will get his magic back."

"Yes," Rachel agreed, brightening at the thought. "But I have to go home in three days, so we don't have long!" As she gazed out at the blue sky, a wisp of silvery mist caught her eye. "Look, that cloud is shaped just like a feather!" she said.

Kirsty looked where Rachel was pointing. "I can't see anything."

Rachel looked again. The wispy shape had vanished. "Perhaps I imagined it," she sighed, turning away to dress.

The memory of the dream fizzed in her tummy like lemonade bubbles.

It felt like a magical start to the day.

She loved staying with Kirsty and sharing fairy adventures with her. The girls had met whilst on holiday on Rainspell Island with their parents.

That was when they had first helped the fairies. On that occasion, Jack Frost had cast a nasty spell to banish the Rainbow Fairies from Fairyland, and the girls had helped all seven of them get safely home.

Rachel and Kirsty hurried down to the kitchen. Mr Tate was sitting at the table. He looked up and smiled at the girls. "Did you sleep well?"

"Yes, thanks," Rachel replied. As she sat down, she saw a bright green notice on the kitchen table. It read, Grand Fun Run at Green Wood Forest, Wetherbury. Everyone welcome. She looked at the date. "That's today."

"Yes. Mum's running in it," said Kirsty.

"Most of the village is taking part. Why don't you two go and watch?" suggested Mr Tate. "You could give Mum some moral support."

"OK," Rachel and Kirsty agreed happily.

Maybe we could look for goblins on the way, thought Rachel. She felt excited, and a bit nervous. Goblins were nasty, tricky things and Jack Frost had cast a spell to make them bigger than normal. Thankfully, fairy law states that nothing can be taller than the King and Queen's fairy castle, so the goblins couldn't get too big. But they still stood nearly as high as Rachel and Kirsty's shoulders.

Mr Tate finished his cup of tea and stood up. "I'm going to pick up Gran and take her to watch the fun run. We might see you there," he told the girls.

"OK, Dad. Goodbye," Kirsty said with a wave.

Just then, Mrs Tate dashed into the kitchen, wearing her jogging kit of shorts, T-shirt and trainers. She smiled at

Kirsty and Rachel. "Sorry, I can't stop, girls. I promised to help mark out the course in the forest."

"That's all right, Mum. We'll follow you up there," Kirsty said.

"We're coming to cheer you on," Rachel explained.

"See you at the woods then!" Mrs Tate called cheerfully as she disappeared out of the door.

A little later, Kirsty and Rachel set out for Green Wood Forest themselves.

"Let's take the river path," Kirsty suggested. "It's a bit longer, but it's much prettier."

"Oh, yes, we might see some ducklings," Rachel agreed eagerly.

As the girls walked up Twisty Lane, sunlight poured through the dancing tree branches and spots of light speckled the road like golden coins. Soon they reached the river. It was very pretty down by the water, where cheerful buttercups dotted the grass and cows grazed happily.

Rachel spotted little puffs of mist rising from the water. "Look! Do you think that could be fairy mist?" she asked.

"I'm not sure," Kirsty replied. "There's often mist round water, isn't there?"

"Oh, yes, especially in the morning and the evening," Rachel remembered. She felt a little disappointed, but brightened when she saw two swans gliding past, followed by three young cygnets. Dragonflies with gossamer wings perched in the reeds beside the sparkling river. "It's a perfect day!" she remarked.

Kirsty nodded. Just ahead she could see the start of the forest. Something was shimmering on a branch of one of the nearer trees. It looked like a ragged silver-grey shawl, glimmering softly in the sunlight.

"What's that?" she asked Rachel.

Rachel went over to have a look. "I don't know, but it's lovely!" she replied. "Just like angel hair for decorating trees at Christmas."

"There's lots more of it on the other branches. Isn't it pretty?" Kirsty touched a strand of the strange, silvery stuff. It clung to her fingers for a moment, before melting away. "It feels cold!" Kirsty shivered, rubbing her hands together.

Rachel leaned forward for a closer
look. Tiny silvery lights shimmered
among the fine, silky threads. "I'm sure
this is fairy mist," she whispered
excitedly.

Kirsty's eyes lit up. "I think you're
right," she agreed. She looked towards
a clump of tall oaks. A wispy cloud of
the strange sparkly mist was building in
the sky and floating gently down
towards the trees. "More fairy mist!"
Kirsty pointed out. "Come on!"

Magic in the Mist

The girls ran towards a stile that led
into the wood. They were out of breath
by the time they jumped down onto the
forest path and looked around. Wispy,
silver mist clung to trees everywhere
and coated the grass with tiny droplets.
Every twig, leaf and flower glowed
and shimmered with a soft silver light.

And where the sunbeams reached down through the trees, the fairy mist sparkled with rainbow light.

"Oh!" breathed Rachel. "It's so beautiful!"

Kirsty stared open-mouthed at the forest. It looked almost as magical as Fairyland itself!

Slowly, the girls moved forward.

After a few steps, Rachel realised that she couldn't see very far ahead.

"This mist is building up fast," she said. "The goblin with the Mist Feather must be hiding really nearby."

Kirsty nodded as thick fog swirled around them. "You're right, Rachel," she agreed. "And we can hardly see a thing. The goblin could be right behind us!"

Rachel rubbed her bare arms and shivered nervously. Only a couple of minutes had passed, but as the mist grew thicker, the forest began to feel dark and unfriendly. Nothing glittered or gleamed anymore. The fog was settling around the girls like a cold blanket.

Shadowy figures moved up ahead. A man wearing a red T-shirt ran out in front of the girls as another runner burst out of the trees. They were heading straight for each other. "Watch out!" called Kirsty. But it was too late. Crash! The runners bumped into each other.

26

"Sorry. Didn't see you there!" one of them said, rubbing his head.

"I've never seen fog like this in summer," replied the other one.

Rachel and Kirsty could hear rustles and bumps all round them. Complaining voices echoed through the fog. Lots of runners were getting lost and having to walk in order to avoid the trees.

"What a shame. This fog is ruining the fun run," said Rachel.

The fog still seemed to be getting thicker. It cloaked the trees in robes of dull grey, making them look dark and sinister.

Suddenly, something caught Kirsty's eye. "Over there!" she pointed.

A bright light was moving towards them, shining like a lantern. Soon the girls could see that it was a tiny gleaming fairy.

"Oh!" gasped Kirsty. "It's Evie the Mist Fairy!"

"Hello again, Rachel and Kirsty," cried Evie in a bright, tinkly voice, as she hovered in the air in front of them. The girls had met Evie in Fairyland, along with all the other Weather Fairies. She had long dark hair and violet eyes. She wore a floaty lilac dress with purple boots, and her wand had a sparkly silver tip from which wisps of shimmering mist drifted constantly.

"Oh, we're so glad to see you!" said Rachel delightedly.

"We really need your help," Kirsty added. "We're sure that the goblin with the Mist Feather isn't far away."

"Yes!" agreed Evie, a frown on her tiny face. "And he's causing lots of misty mischief!"

"Could you leave a magic trail behind
us, as we go further into the woods?"
Rachel asked. "Then we can look for
the goblin and still find our way back
to the stile and out."

Evie grinned. She waved her wand and
a fountain of fairy dust shot out. It
floated to the ground and
formed a glittering path.
"Of course, now
we won't get
lost!" she said.
"But we might
bump into the
runners," Kirsty
pointed out. "Let's
turn ourselves into
fairies, Rachel,
then we can fly."

The Fairy Queen had given Rachel and Kirsty beautiful golden lockets full of fairy dust. The girls sprinkled themselves with the magic dust and soon shrank to fairy size. The trees seemed as big as giants' castles looming out of the thick fog.

"I love being a fairy!" Kirsty sang out happily.

Rachel twisted round to look over her shoulder. There were her fairy wings on her back, shining and delicate.

"Hooray!" Evie rose into the air, a trail of glittering mist streaming from her wand, and the two girls followed her deeper into the forest.

Below them, the runners were s
stumbling about in the fog. "Poor
Mum. She was really looking forward
to today. That nasty goblin's spoiling
everyone's fun," said Kirsty crossly.

Suddenly, Rachel spotted a dark,
hunched shape in the mist below. She
waved urgently to Kirsty and Evie.
"Look down there," she called softly.
"I think we've found the goblin!"

Goblin in the Fog

They all floated down to investigate.
The mist was heavier here and sticky. It
dragged at Rachel's wings as she flew
through it. "Oh, it's not a goblin – it's
just a dead tree," she sighed, landing
on the thick twisted trunk. She felt
disappointed. The dark, squat shape had
looked just like a goblin from the air.

35

"We may not have found him yet," Kirsty whispered to her friend, "but I still think that goblin's nearby. The mist here smells nasty and musty and it's harder to fly through."

Rachel fluttered her beautiful shiny wings. "Yes," she agreed. "It's like cold porridge."

Just then, they heard a gruff, complaining voice. "It's not fair! I'm cold and I'm lost and I'm hungry!" There was a loud sniff, like a pig snorting. "Poor me!"

Rachel, Kirsty, and Evie looked at each other in excitement.

"That's definitely a goblin speaking!" declared Evie.

"Quick! Let's hide in that tree before he sees us," suggested Rachel.

They flew upwards to land on the branch of a huge oak and peered down through the thick green leaves. Sure enough, the goblin sat on a log below them. They could see the top of his head and his enormous bony feet. They could also hear a horrible gurgling sound, like slimy stuff going down a plughole.

"Lost in this horrible forest! And I'm so hungry," moaned the goblin, clutching his rumbling tummy. "I'd love some toadstool stew and worm dumplings!" Suddenly he jumped up.

"What was that? Who's there?" He peered up into the tree's branches. Rachel, Kirsty and Evie quickly darted behind the oak leaves and after a moment the goblin sank down onto his log again. "Must have been a squirrel," he muttered. "I want to go home!"

The girls could see the goblin clearly now. He had bulging, crossed eyes and a big, lumpy nose like a potato.

His arms were long and skinny but he had short legs and knobbly knees.

"Look what he's holding!" whispered Evie.

Kirsty and Rachel peered through the leaves and saw that a beautiful silvery feather with a lilac tip was clutched in the goblin's stubby fingers. "The Mist Feather!" the girls exclaimed together.

Then Rachel frowned. "If the goblin's lost in the fog, why doesn't he use the magic feather to get rid of it?" she asked.

"Because he doesn't know how," Evie explained. "He's waving the feather about all over the place without thinking – but by doing so he's only making more and more mist."

It was true. The goblin was shaking the Mist Feather and mumbling to himself sorrowfully as thick swirls of fog drifted around him. "Earwig fritters, beetle pancakes, lovely slug sandwiches…" he muttered.

Just then, one of the runners passed close by. The goblin shot to his feet and hid behind a tree. He was trembling so much that the three friends could hear his knees knocking together. "It's a…it's a Pogwurzel!" he whispered in panic.

As the sound of the runner's footsteps faded, the goblin peeped out. "Phew! The Pogwurzel's gone." He flopped back down on the log, but carried on looking about him nervously.

Kirsty turned to Evie. "What is a Pogwurzel?" she asked.

Evie smiled, her violet eyes sparkling. "Pogwurzels are strange, magical, goblin-chasing monsters!" she replied.

Rachel looked at the fairy curiously. "Where do they live?" She and Kirsty had been to Fairyland a few times now. They had seen elves, goblins and all kinds of fairies – but never a Pogwurzel.

Evie gave a peal of silvery laughter. "Nowhere!" she said. "Because they don't exist! You see goblin children can be really naughty, so their mothers tell them that if they don't do as they're told, a Pogwurzel will come and chase them!"

Kirsty and Rachel laughed so much they nearly fell off the branch.

Then Rachel suddenly turned to Kirsty and Evie in excitement. "I've got an idea," she whispered, her eyes shining. "I think I know how we can get the Mist Feather back!"

The Pogwurzel Plot

Evie and Kirsty stared at Rachel. "Tell us!" they pleaded.

Rachel outlined her plan. "If we can convince the goblin that the forest is full of Pogwurzels, he'll do anything to escape. He's bound to want the mist cleared away, so he can find his way out of the wood.

Since he's too stupid to work out how to use the Mist Feather to clear the fog, maybe we can persuade him to give the feather to Evie and let her try."

Evie clapped her hands together in delight. "Then I can keep it and take it back to Doodle!" she said. "It's a brilliant plan!"

"But I'm not sure how we can make the goblin think that there are hundreds of Pogwurzels in the forest," Rachel added.

The three friends racked their brains. Kirsty thought of her mum and the other runners trying to find their way around the fun run course. That gave her an idea of her own. "I know just how we can convince the goblin about Pogwurzels," she cried. "Evie, if you make us human-sized again, Rachel and I can creep up on the goblin from behind, then run past him, screaming that a Pogwurzel is chasing us!"

"Yes, that could work," Evie agreed.

"We'll have to be very convincing," Rachel put in.

Evie nodded. "But you two can do it.
I know you can," she said encouragingly.
The three friends flew silently down to
the ground behind the oak tree. Evie
waved her wand and the
girls zoomed up to
their normal height.
"Ready?"asked Kirsty.
"You bet," Rachel
replied firmly.
The girls crept
towards the goblin.
They could see
him sitting on
his log, still
muttering to himself.
"Now!" hissed Rachel.
Kirsty dashed forward. "Help! Help!
Save us from the Pogwurzel!" she shouted.

48

Rachel ran after her. "It's huge and scary and won't leave us alone!" she cried.

The goblin leapt to his feet, his eyes like saucers. "What?" he gasped. "Who are you?"

Kirsty stopped. "Oh, my goodness, a goblin in Pogwurzel Wood!" she exclaimed, pretending to be surprised.

Rachel stopped too. "You must be very brave," she declared.

The goblin's crossed-eyes flicked from Rachel to Kirsty. "Why?" he demanded shakily. "Are their many Pogwurzels around here?"

"Oh, yes," Kirsty chimed in. "Hundreds. This forest is full of them. One of them was chasing us just now," she added, looking nervously over her shoulder. "He'll be along soon I should think."

Just then, Evie fluttered down, her wings shining in the fog. "Pogwurzels especially love to catch goblins, you know. I've heard that they cook them and eat them," she said.

"Eat them!" the goblin's face turned pale with fear.

"Oh, yes. If I was you, I'd get out of this wood right now," Evie went on.

"But I can't," wailed the goblin. "I've lost my way. The fog is so thick I can hardly see my own bony toes!"

Evie smiled. "I'll help you," she said sweetly. "Just give me that feather you're holding and I'll magic a clear pathway out of the forest for you."

Kirsty and Rachel hardly dared breathe. Their plan was working so far, but what would the goblin do next?

He pinched his nose thoughtfully. "I don't know. Jack Frost won't like it if I give you the Mist Feather."

"But he's not the one being chased by a Pogwurzel, is he?" Rachel pointed out quickly. "He's not the one who'll be roasted and toasted and turned into Goblin Pie!"

"The Pogwurzels in this wood are extra-enormous," Kirsty put in. "And really, really fierce."

"So is Jack Frost," the goblin said, looking sullen. "I think I'll keep the feather."

Kirsty's heart sank. It looked like the goblin was more stubborn than they had expected. She exchanged looks with Rachel. Now what could they do?

Goblin Pie

Evie hovered close to the girls. "I've got an idea," she whispered. "You distract the goblin, so he won't notice what I'm doing."

"What are you all talking about?" demanded the goblin suspiciously.

"We think we heard another Pogwurzel," Kirsty replied.

"Where?" the goblin spun round anxiously.

While his back was turned, Evie waved her wand in a complicated pattern. A big fountain of silver and violet sparks shot into a nearby bush, carrying fairy magic there.

"I can hear it! It's coming this way!"
Rachel called to the goblin.

"Don't believe you," the goblin
sneered. "I can't hear it. You're just
trying to scare me. I bet you
never even saw a Pogwurzel
in the first place."

"Listen properly
for yourself then,"
Evie said.

The goblin put
his head on one
side and frowned
in concentration.
Kirsty and Rachel
waited. They weren't sure
exactly what Evie had planned.

Suddenly a deep, scary roar came
from the centre of the nearby bush.

"Raaghh! I'm a ferocious Pogwurzel! And I really fancy Goblin Pie for my supper!"

"Wow! Evie's magical voice is really scary," Kirsty whispered to Rachel.

The goblin stiffened. "Help me, Mummy!" he cried. "A Pogwurzel wants to eat me! I'm sorry I put those toenail clippings in your bed. I won't do it again. Help!" He stumbled behind Kirsty and Rachel, trying to hide. "Don't eat me, Mr Pogwurzel. Eat these girls

58

instead. I bet they taste sweeter than me!"
Evie's magical trick voice came from
the bush again. "I only eat
goblins," it boomed.
"Especially really
naughty ones
– like you!"
The goblin
squealed in
alarm and his
eyes bulged.
He took the
Mist Feather
from his belt and
thrust it at Evie.
"Make the mist go
away so I can get out of
here," he begged. "I don't
want to be made into Goblin Pie!"

Evie gave a joyful smile, took the feather and waved it expertly in the air. A clear path immediately appeared through the mist. The goblin gave a final terrified glance over his shoulder and then ran away as fast as he could, his big feet flapping noisily.

Kirsty, Rachel and Evie laughed merrily.

"Evie, that trick voice was brilliant!" Rachel said.

"It even scared me!" laughed Kirsty.

"And now we have the Mist Feather!" Evie declared, waving it over her head.

Silver sparks shot into
the air and the mist
began to fade.
Moments later, the
sun shone down
onto the forest again.

Rachel and Kirsty beamed.
"We can give another magic feather
back to Doodle!" Rachel said happily.

Evie flew up and did a little twirl in
the air for joy. Silver and violet mist
sparkled all around her.

"And the fun run should be easier
going now," Kirsty put in. "Let's go
and see if we can spot Mum before we
head home to Doodle."

Back on Course

The three friends made their way towards the fun run course.

The bracken and forest paths were touched with gold, and the smell of earth and green leaves filled the air. Runners pounded along between trees marked with big red signs. Everyone could see where they were going now.

"You'd better hide on my shoulder," Rachel said to Evie.

Evie nodded and fluttered beneath Rachel's hair.

Suddenly, Kirsty spotted her mum dashing through the trees. Two other runners were close on her heels.

"Come on, Mum!" Kirsty shouted.

"You can do it!" yelled Rachel.

Kirsty's mum threw them a brief smile and waved. "Not far to go now," she called.

Kirsty and Rachel jumped up and down with delight. Evie cheered too, but only Rachel could hear her silvery voice.

"Looks like your mum's doing well," said a voice at Kirsty's side.

"Dad! Gran! You're here!" Kirsty exclaimed.

"Only just in time. That fog held us up," said Mr Tate. "Strange how it's completely disappeared now. Almost like magic."

Rachel and Kirsty looked at each other and smiled.

"We're going to head home now," Kirsty told her dad.

"Right you are," he replied. "We'll go and wait for Mum at the finish line."

On the way home, the girls revelled in the glorious sunshine, but Kirsty couldn't help missing the sparkly fairy mist just a little bit.

"Time to give Doodle his feather back," said Rachel, as they reached Kirsty's cottage. "I wonder if he'll speak

to us again." Every time the girls had returned a tail feather, Doodle had sprung briefly to life and started to speak. He'd given them part of a message and they were keen to hear the rest.

"I hope so," said Kirsty. She repeated what Doodle had said so far. "Beware! Jack Frost will come…"

Evie flew up to the barn roof. As she slotted the feather into place, the girls watched eagerly.

A fountain of copper and gold sparks fizzed from Doodle's tail. The rusty old weather-vane disappeared and in its place blazed a fiery magic cockerel. Doodle fluffed up his glorious feathers and turned to stare at Rachel and Kirsty. "If his—" he squawked. But before he could finish the message, his feathers turned to iron and he became an ordinary weather-vane again.

Kirsty frowned. "Beware! Jack Frost will come if his…" she said, putting together all the words Doodle had said so far.

"Jack Frost will come if his what?" queried Rachel curiously.

Kirsty shook her head. "We'll just have to find the next feather and hope Doodle can tell us," she sighed.

Evie nodded. "It's important to know the whole message. Jack Frost is dangerous," she warned. "And now I must leave you." She hugged Rachel and Kirsty in turn. "Dear friends. Thank you for helping me."

"You're welcome," said Kirsty.

"Say hello to all our friends in Fairyland for us," added Rachel.

"I will," Evie promised, as she zoomed up into the brilliant blue sky. Her wand fizzed trails of silver mist, then she was gone.

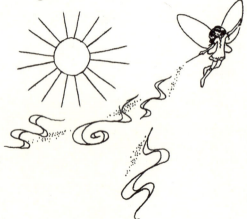

Kirsty chuckled. "I've just remembered something the goblin said. I wonder whose toenail clippings he put in his mum's bed!" she said.

Rachel laughed happily. What an exciting day it had been and there were still two days of her holiday left!

The Weather Fairies

Crystal, Abigail, Pearl, Goldie and
Evie have got their feathers back.
Now Rachel and Kirsty must help
Storm the Lightning Fairy

Magic in the Air

"I can't believe tomorrow is my last day here," groaned Rachel Walker. She was staying for a week's holiday with her friend, Kirsty Tate, at the Tates' house in Wetherbury. The girls had had so many adventures together, they knew it was going to be difficult to say goodbye.

They were walking to the park, keen
to get outside now the rain had
stopped. It had been pouring down all
night, but now the sun was shining.

"Put your coats on, though, won't
you?" Mrs Tate had told them before
they set off. "It looks quite breezy out
there."

"It's been such fun, having you to
stay," Kirsty told her friend.
"I don't think I'll ever forget this week,
will you?"

Rachel shook her head. "No way,"
she agreed firmly.

The two friends smiled at each other.
It had been a very busy week. A snowy,
windy, cloudy, sunny, misty week
– thanks to Jack Frost and his naughty
goblins. The goblins had stolen the seven

magic tail feathers from Doodle, the
Fairyland weather cockerel, and taken
one each into the human world. The
feathers were used by the weather fairies
to control the weather so the goblins
were stirring up all kinds of trouble!

Rachel and Kirsty were helping the
Weather Fairies to get the feathers
back. Without them Doodle was just an
ordinary iron weather-vane! Kirsty's
dad had found him lying in the park
after he'd chased the goblins into the
human world. He brought him home to
put him on the roof of the old barn.

"Doodle's got five of his magic
feathers back now. But I do hope we
find the last two before you have to go
home," Kirsty said, pushing open the
park gates.

Rachel nodded, but before she could say anything, there was a pattering sound and raindrops started splashing down.

The girls looked up in dismay to see a huge purple storm cloud covering the sun. The sky was darkening by the second and the rain was falling more and more heavily.

"Quick!" Kirsty shouted. "Before we get soaked!"

Win a Rainbow Magic Sparkly T-Shirt and Goody Bag!

In every book in the Rainbow Magic Weather series (books 8-14) there is a hidden picture of a magic feather with a secret letter in it. Find all seven letters and re-arrange them to make a special Fairyland word, then send it to us. Each month we will put the entries into a draw. The winner will receive a Rainbow Magic Sparkly T-shirt and Goody Bag!

Send your entry on a postcard to Rainbow Magic Competition, Orchard Books, 96 Leonard Street, London EC2A 4XD. Australian readers should write to 32/45-51 Huntley Street, Alexandria, NSW 2015. Don't forget to include your name and address.

FERN THE GREEN FAIRY
1-84362-019-7

SAFFRON THE YELLOW FAIRY
1-84362-018-9

AMBER THE ORANGE FAIRY
1-84362-017-0

RUBY THE RED FAIRY
1-84362-016-2

HEATHER THE VIOLET FAIRY
1-84362-022-7

IZZY THE INDIGO FAIRY
1-84362-021-9

SKY THE BLUE FAIRY
1-84362-020-0

The Weather Fairies

CRYSTAL THE SNOW FAIRY
1-84362-633-0

ABIGAIL THE BREEZE FAIRY
1-84362-634-9

PEARL THE CLOUD FAIRY
1-84362-635-7

GOLDIE THE SUNSHINE FAIRY
1-84362-641-1

EVIE THE MIST FAIRY
1-84362-636-5

STORM THE LIGHTNING FAIRY
1-84362-637-3

HAYLEY THE RAIN FAIRY
1-84362-638-1

Collect all of the Rainbow Magic books!

RAINBOW magic

by Daisy Meadows

Ruby the Red Fairy	ISBN	1 84362 016 2
Amber the Orange Fairy	ISBN	1 84362 017 0
Saffron the Yellow Fairy	ISBN	1 84362 018 9
Fern the Green Fairy	ISBN	1 84362 019 7
Sky the Blue Fairy	ISBN	1 84362 020 0
Izzy the Indigo Fairy	ISBN	1 84362 021 9
Heather the Violet Fairy	ISBN	1 84362 022 7

The Weather Fairies

Crystal the Snow Fairy	ISBN	1 84362 633 0
Abigail the Breeze Fairy	ISBN	1 84362 634 9
Pearl the Cloud Fairy	ISBN	1 84362 635 7
Goldie the Sunshine Fairy	ISBN	1 84362 641 1
Evie the Mist Fairy	ISBN	1 84362 636 5
Storm the Lightning Fairy	ISBN	1 84362 637 3
Hayley the Rain Fairy	ISBN	1 84362 638 1

All priced at £3.99
Rainbow Magic books are available from all good bookshops,
or can be ordered direct from the publisher:
Orchard Books, PO BOX 29, Douglas IM99 1BQ
Credit card orders please telephone 01624 836000
or fax 01624 837033 or visit our Internet site: www.wattspub.co.uk
or e-mail: bookshop@enterprise.net for details.

To order please quote title, author and ISBN
and your full name and address.
Cheques and postal orders should be made payable to 'Bookpost plc.'
Postage and packing is FREE within the UK
(overseas customers should add £1.00 per book).

Prices and availability are subject to change.